CLOWN
Quentin Blake

A Tom Maschler Book
JONATHAN CAPE
London

for Christine

First published 1995

1 3 5 7 9 10 8 6 4 2

© Quentin Blake 1995

Quentin Blake has asserted his right under
the Copyright, Designs and Patents Act 1988
to be identified as the author of this work

First published in the United Kingdom in 1995 by
Jonathan Cape, Random House, 20 Vauxhall Bridge Road,
London SW1V 2SA

Random House UK Limited Reg. No. 954009

A CIP catalogue record for this book
is available from the British Library

ISBN O 224 04510 5

Printed in Hong Kong